THE BLACKBOARD

Dive into the past

KRIPPASHINI T.

Noel Lorenz House of Fiction

www.noellorenz.com

Title of Book: *The Blackboard*
Author of Book: Krippashini T.
First Published in India in Dec 2021 by Noel Lorenz House of Fiction
Copyright © Krippashini T., 2021.

ISBN 13: 978-93-93695-31-4
Published and Printed By
Noel Lorenz House of Fiction
Headquarters - Kolkata, West Bengal, India
154A, KCG Road, Kolkata - 700050
www.noellorenz.com

Dive into the past

About the Book

What does your mind get striked with, when you think of,

THE BLACKBOARD?

•He passed by her classroom everyday just to catch a glimpse of her.

However, she never knew about the secret admirer.

•I was bread and she was my jam. We were the best pair to be thought....

Yet, I was toasted

And she often went stolen from the jar.

Millions of disappearing visitors,

Deforming the lives through white scribbles.

Letters may fade but knowledge will never.

Where your partner becomes chalk and duster,

Leaders attach to like a moth.

To be with you everyone happily come forth! - THE BLACKBOARD!!

———-Dive into past————

Dive into the past

About the Author

Krippashini Thiagarajan

She is pursuing her Bachelor's in Dental Surgery at Karpaga Vinayaga Institution, Tamilnadu, India.

Her interest in English keeps on gradually increasing as she comes through more and more workpieces, chances, and platforms.

She did her schooling at Srinivasa Matriculation Hr. Sec. School, the place which served her with ecstatic knacks for English.

She is the co-author of the anthologies:

1. Impetus of life

2. Stop regretting and Start living

Dive into the past

3. Broke N beautiful

4. Kallistê

5. Khwaishen

6. Manifestations of Love

7. Women Empowerment

Her workpiece on another fiction is to be released soon.

She nourishes 'Incrediblewritings', her Instagram page with interesting genres.

To become an ethical and successful doctor, she is undergoing studies to continue her PG.

DOB: 02.12.2000 at Trichy, Tamilnadu, India.

Contact info: tkapple34 @ gmail.com

Instagram: @ krippashini @ incrediblewritings

Dive into the past

Contents

Dive into the past

The Broken Particles

10.06.1834 - On this day, Thomas Babington Macaulay, a former British secretary at war, arrived in India. On a surprising note, India is the only country in world history that has its both education system and Indian Penal Code designed by the same person. It was Macaulay. Maybe he would have thought both are the same. That's why our classrooms look like a prisoner's cell and our schools a prison.

For fifteen years of schooling, I had successfully learnt how to be a perfect slave. A slave who looks up to the Himalayas wonders and says, 'How beautiful Mt. Everest is!' A slave who doesn't have independent thoughts.

My teachers made us 'mark minded'. And we became 'money minded'.

We are birds. My school never taught us 'How to fly'. It taught us 'How not to fly'. And the result is our feathers have broken.

Our school makes us a machine. A machine that doesn't know what humanity is.

Our books were very busy planting knowledge in our minds. But it failed to tell us to pour water every day.

We had studied 'Books are good companions', but had never visited the library even once in our school life.

Dive into the past

My school has seen thousands of students like me dreaming, 'One day everyone says I'm one in thousand' But in reality, I'm one among those thousand.

"Dear School, don't be proud in saying you are the best in showing 100% pass results. Because we know how much you care about below average students by sending them to private coaching centres."

"Dear class teacher, please stop saying that we are the best batch you have ever seen in your teaching career. Because we know you have said this even to the previous batches and will repeat this same to the upcoming batches too."

I remember my maths teacher would always call me to solve complex problems on the board. When I couldn't solve, she would clearly explain each and every step to derive the answer. But she never knew that I didn't understand the question itself.

Whenever we made noise, our teacher used to ask, 'Do you think you are all in a market!?' And now I know the answer. 'We were in the market which sells education. The sellers were clever. The buyers were ignorant.'

The roll numbers are not just numerical. It separated my friend and me from sitting next to each other in the exam hall.

Whenever someone compares me with others, I will remember the broken leg of the wooden bench I used to sit in my classroom. Every time I would keep a paper ball under the fractured leg. But the next day, I won't even find the ball in the dustbin.

Dive into the past

I'm sure during the alumni meet, our teachers would easily remember everyone's names except us. We are the middle benchers. They won't even recognise our faces.

We (The boys) would always hide our ID cards in our shirt pockets because we were always dissatisfied with our faces in the ID cards. We never wanted to show it to others.

Luckily, our teachers had never visited us during our lunchtime discussions. If they were, they would have got disappointed by knowing their nicknames.

I was the only unlucky person in my entire class because my birthday was on the 1st of January. I had never celebrated my birthdays in school. Not even once.

Our school memories fade away when we couldn't recollect the day when we got our first punishment.

The first rank holders are always less smart than others who perfectly put their parent's signature in the progress report.

It's been four years since I left my school. But every Friday, even now, the curiosity of knowing 'whether Saturday is a holiday!?' remains in my heart.

All my class timetables had four PT periods in all the weeks. But it exists only in the timetables.

Four palanquin bearers once carried Macaulay on their shoulders and walked for four hundred miles. And I, as an Indian student, carried him for fifteen years on my back, just like carrying my school bag.

Dive into the past

Finally, Macaulay took us as a chalk piece and wrote his name on the 'History Board'. And now, we are broken into small particles.

- Nithese Krishna.

Dive into the past

Mole

Madam, what was the biggest challenge that you faced in the journey to this achievement?"
The question came from the girls' section of the audience. The whole auditorium went silent, expecting a long list of hurdles.
Smiling, I switched on my mike.
"To be myself. And now I know, trying not to be, was the biggest mistake I had ever committed."
I am not sure how many of them understood what I meant. Anyway, they gave me a huge round of applause.
The function was over. With the help of the organising committee members and the security officers, I somehow managed to get into the car. It was then I remembered the memento they gave me. I took it out of the bag.
'Continue to inspire generations.'
With Love,
St Mary's Arts & Science college

I was thinking of taking a nap before I reached home. It has been so long since I visited my parents. They would have invited all the relatives home; I guess after I confirmed about my visit today.
They are so proud about Gowry Lakshmi I.A.S., but they were not, about the little girl who aspired to become an IAS officer, determined to work hard and

Dive into the past

succeed. Unlike my elder brother, they were always worried about how I did not inherit their fair skin tone. They were worried about who will marry me and the extra dowry they should be giving to compensate for my dark skin colour. They always ensured my brother was given preference in everything at home, right from the number of chicken pieces to ambitions and career.

They were least bothered about my education and me as well unless someone initiated a discussion about my marriage. As a child, I used to think that the white letters on the blackboard were bold and beautiful only because of the black background. Thus I hoped that all these bitter experiences would lead me to a bright future.

When I completed my 12th standard, I was 17 years old, one year young, to get married legally. I guess that is the reason why they allowed me to go to college. My home, where I never felt like home, left me in loneliness and insecurity. This became the reason for me to develop a forever relationship with books. Also, I loved to pen down my thoughts. If I ever publish it as a book, I will name it 'GRIEF', synonymous with my childhood.

The endless love for books made me choose Literature, the best decision of my life. Three years of college brought out the blooming poet and story writer in me. I met people with whom I could connect and talk for hours without getting tired.

The most important among them was Mrs Anitha, my professor, who never behaved like one. She was

Dive into the past

a best friend, mentor and mother to me. I felt home could be a person too, after meeting her.

She always used to say," Keep your journals safe, we will publish it once you become Gowry Lakshmi IAS."

Her voice managed to replace my mothers' voice that echoed inside me since childhood.

"Gowry, hereafter you should not play outside. You are no longer a kid."

"Why do you always choose dark shades to wear? It makes you even darker."

"Learn cooking and household chores before marriage. What are you even going to do with all these story books?"

Graduation also meant the end of the golden days of life; I was left alone once again, in the dark corners of my house. I was unaware of the serious discussions about my marriage and that it was almost fixed. My willingness was not at all a matter of concern.

One fine morning, a young man in formals arrived in a red Maruthi car. He appeared like a prince in a chariot to my family, so kind to marry a girl with a darker skin tone than him.

His parents and sister scanned me from top to bottom and concluded that despite being dusky, I am beautiful. My family took it as a great compliment, but I knew that was just a reminder of the so-called sacrifice they do. None of them asked me what my ambition was or if I was ready for this.

Dive into the past

My husband's home was a great experience for how narrow-minded people can ever be. They needed a free maid and cook. Forget Civil services; I could not touch a book for months. I felt like I was having a nightmare, and I will get over it one day. But nothing happened. I managed to get through his dominating character and racist comments, but then it worsened that he started the physical assault.

I came to know that I was pregnant. I hoped to get some rest, and he would love me after this. But nothing changed.

I got tired. I was tired of wiping tears. I was tired of hating myself. I was tired of pleading. I decided to face my fears. My fear of living alone. My fear of what people will say if I go for a divorce. Whenever I complained about my husband, my mother always tried to convince me that all these were normal and I should adjust. The next step will be emotional blackmail. But I did not care. I decided to fight for myself.

Nothing was easy. Physical pains were bearable. But my mental health was seriously affected. Anitha mam came to save me, once again. She took me to her home, looked after me, helped me file a divorce, and motivated me to start reading again. I gave birth to Nila. Mam became her grandma and took care of her when I studied. She made me realise that I deserved happier days, and I am good enough to make it possible.

When the media celebrated my victory, I got calls from my family, who dumped me long back and

Dive into the past

cursed me for destroying their reputation. I did not want to go. But Anitha mam compelled me to go and meet them. She asked me to take Nila with me, but I did not.

I do not want my daughter to get judged based on her gender, skin colour or whatever.

I don't want to raise her as a girl who stays silent facing injustice.

It took me 22 years and a lot of horrible experiences to discover my inner strength. I don't want that to happen to my child.

I want her to accept herself right from childhood and grow up as a brave girl aware of her abilities.

I want her to live her life to the fullest, inspiring generations.

- Ashwathy.

Dive into the past

Hi Black Board"

Millions of disappearing visitors,
Deforming the lives through white scribbles.
Impossible to see you in May,
Where the duet of black and white chills,
Proud to decorate you with colours,
Literate consider you as the main path.
Letters may fade, but knowledge never fade,
Jumping from you to the bin brain.
Being the centre of attraction from all corners,
On occasion, every stroke drain.
Where your partner becomes chalk and duster,
Leaders attach to like a moth.
To be with being you, everyone, happily come forth.

- SUVI. M

Dive into the past

Silent Successor!

People need me though I'm dark and silent,
Nothing could be done if I'm gone,
Future leaders cannot be formed,
Hope for the future is in my right hands.
White is white only when written on me.
I lie from east to west,
Extremely kept quiet during the test.
Facing every face in the morning,
Demolishing white chalk with my rugged behaviour,
Yet, I battle between classroom fights,
Leaders sticking on to me with feeling proudest,
Holding every subject till being taken.
Everyone gets a nap except me,
Even to cleanse me to need to reach height,
Yes- I'm black, stubborn, ugly after use.
But I shower rays of wisdom through me,
Standing as the centre of concentration key.

- SUVI. M

Dream Big!

Entering the gates of sixteen, Susana started to hate going to school. She was the topper of the class; every teacher wished to have a student like her. Learning was her first and last workday on a daily basis. Her classmates tried to win over her proficiency, yet she conquered and was a shining star. When days started to pass by, she sometimes refused and never showed interest to go to school. Her parent thought she was losing interest in her studies and thus behaving like this. But it wasn't the truth. Susana gradually sloped down from the top ranks, which gave a surprise to everyone. She began to play and spent most of her time doing idle jobs. Finally, she began to fail in her subjects, especially Math, which was once her favourite subject. Securing centum was an easy calk but what made her behave like this was a million-dollar question to everyone around her.

One fine day, when Susana's mother sat beside her and gave advice. She was so soft to listen and didn't give any clue about the truth behind her behaviour. Time was flying by; Susana began to tell the truth for her rugged behaviour. Susana said to her that we came up from a middle-class family where everything could not be brought immediately. They live a perfect money life where they can neither spend nor save. So when Susana looks at the blackboard in her class for listening, she knows she

Dive into the past

studies well, she is capable of anything, and everything could afford every mark. Her imagination of dreaming big made her behave so. Susana explained to her mother that if she studied well, secured high scores, and wanted to enrol herself in INDIAN SPACE RESEARCH ORGANISATION or do medicine, we wouldn't be able to afford so much. The studies she is learning make her think for a better tomorrow, but in reality, they aren't well enough to plan the next day's meal. What if I secure the highest score and cannot go for higher studies? Then it makes me go deep down the earth. It's better not to take good marks at the initial stage rather than to feel late. The blackboard of my class is inducing me to dream bigger and bigger, but the blackboard doesn't know our financial status, mommy, what a dumb board, mommy, she wept. Though it gains knowledge every day, it doesn't understand personal happenings. This was Susana's reason for her strange behaviour. After hearing all her reasons, Susana's mother took a deep breath and sipped water.

Well, my pretty daughter, listen to me, she said, patting her. Susana lived a legend named Dr. APJ Abdul Kalam, who was loved by all, especially students. He believed that students are the pillars of nature, and to add, he believed especially the backbencher students, which ordinary people doesn't. He was mad at student and their career. He was born in a very middle-class family but made the whole world look at him even now. So imagine that

Dive into the past

he is with you and talking to you through the blackboard Susana. He once said that "black color is sentimentally bad but every black board makes the students life bright ". It is a shame that a student cannot colour the future when you have beautiful shades. And also, keep in mind, success cannot be afforded but need to be built through the stones of hard work, patience and goals. It is the true value we give to such a man. Live your life and make his name great.

That is the day when Susana took her axe of learning again and started to shine as she was before. She often spoke to the blackboard as it gave her dreams. Never underestimate anything unless it is established.
- SUVI. M

Dive into the past

The Broken Soul

Everyone needs a good listener,

to open their wounded soul!

"You are not worth for our friendship! Who wants to befriend a nerd like you!? Have you seen yourself? You are a looser! You are a mistake! Do you get that. Looser!". Avantika woke up from her dream. She is drenched with her sweat. Tears are flowing without her consent. As always, she wants the day to end! She wants to end her misery! But the question is when!?

Like her name, she is a blossom with chubby cheeks. Loving and caring. A cute chatterbox. A girl with willpower. She loves to compete. Crying is not her cup of tea. She loves challenges. Welcomes failure whole heartedly. The Apple of her family. Every day blabbering to her mother about her daily activities. Always plaster a smile on her lips.

School life is a paradise for many. But not for Avantika. For her, it's just a place where you can complete your studies. She did not reach this conclusion just like that. Her experience and situation demands. She used to believe that her friends loved her, would support her. But not everyone's assumption is true. Yes, assumption. She thought, she believed, but actually, these are her assumptions. To be precise, false assumptions.

Dive into the past

They used her for their own benefit. Their own selfish purpose. Students speak behind her back. They would make fun of her appearance. They humiliate her as a nerd. They broke her from inside. She thought the fault is on her side, and she decided to rectify them. She changed herself for others. She started to bully herself, so may that fact could bring her so-called friends. Though she portrays herself as strong, but her heart is so weak than a cardiac patient.

She does every damn thing to be a perfect daughter. But all she got in return was humiliation. She loves dancing. But she crushed her dreams for her parents. Because they thought it was for her goodwill, as it affects her studies, they do what is the best for her. Not according to her wish. They provide what she needs but not what she wants. She does every single thing she asks to do, even against her wish. Just to see the happiness in her parents' face. She tries her best to score better marks. But her parents always want her to top her exams.

Everything changed. She is not the same lovely girl who leads a carefree life. Time is the best healer. But for her, time taught her a good lesson. Her smile does not reach her eyes. There is always a longing in her eyes that fails to be noticed. She mastered masking her emotions. She started to ignore the taunting. She started distancing herself from everyone. She is not ready to break the already broken soul. She feared to trust someone.

Dive into the past

This is not her. Definitely not her nature. She is so naïve to trust everyone blindly.

Every night she will cry her heart out, eventually drift to sleep. But her sleep only lasts for a few hours. She was awake from her nightmare. Where all the horrible things which she went through again projected in her mind. Her heart says to move on; still, more are there to face. But her fifteen-year broken soul ignores the begging. She wants to open up to her parents. But she knows they would blame her for that. They will ask her to concentrate on her studies, which are more important than herimmature thoughts. She hates that. She hates to be blamed for everything; she does not even involve. She hates that she is always being left alone in the end. She hates that she is still depending on others for love. In the process of finding love in others, she failed to love herself. She lost the trust in people. She lost faith in the truth.

Every person's life depends on the way they grow up. Their attitude and approach towards their life depend on the atmosphere they face. Negligence and ignorance ruined her childhood. Depression overpowers her confidence. She feared that she would be left alone for her whole life. She wants a shoulder to cry and comfort. Love, this is what her heart longed for. She wants to know how good it feels to be loved and cared for! She wants someone to heal her broken soul!

- Yuvarani.

Dive into the past

A Dream

The school bus finally arrived.

Professor Aadi has been waiting for a while.

"Ah! Finally," he thought.

Mr. Aadi stepped inside the bus. Though he didn't meet everyone eye to eye, he felt a sense of drowsiness coming from everyone.

He spotted a corner seat at the second last row.

The drowsiness spread through the air like a wildfire and put him to sleep like a cat as soon as the bus left the stop. Immediately, he was put in a dream state. Usually, the dreams were fascinating and adventurous, but when he started working as a professor in this school, his dreams were only related to one incident from his past.

The dream goes like.

"Get up! Get up! Get up!!!" his mom shouted. (Funny, he was sleeping in his dream also as a result of the hectic life in reality.)

The 12 years old Aadi woke up asking for coffee, half asleep. His mom was busy packing the lunch for her husband and her beloved son. Although with a lot of things happening around his mom, she gave him the coffee with just a simple smile.

Dive into the past

"Go. Take a bath. It's late for school." his mom hurriedly requested.

It was a rainy season. The water stayed wherever it was allowed to. His house only has a solar heater because of his environmentalist father. This made it difficult to heat water during the rainy season. He took a refreshing cold shower that woke him immediately from the half-sleep state.

He dusted off his bicycle. By the time his friend Karn has arrived at his house. They both reached the school at a surprisingly perfect time. As they both were walking in the hallway, the most beautiful girl from their class or their entire school, "according to them," was running towards them. As she passed Aadi, her skirt which, was floating in the air, kissed his forearm. Aadi's eye dilated as soon as it happened, and he was bragging about it to his friend throughout their journey to their classroom.

"OMG! Don't touch my hand. I will preserve it till my last breath." Aadi told his friend as they sat together in their bench.

While the teacher took the attendance, a crooked teethed and the eyed girl came in wearing spectacles that didn't suit her uneven face.

"Dude!! Is she a new joinee?" Aadi told Karn in an unpleasant tone.

The weather was filled with anxiety of thunder and lighting as Aadi peeked outside the window.

Dive into the past

"I guess so." Karn replied.

After two whole periods of meaningless words coming out from their teachers, the break bell rang. This alerted the boys, and they instantly ran towards the canteen. Even though they were as early as possible, the token area was crowded like houseflies all-around a peeled jackfruit. A friend of Karn was almost close to the token area. They threw the money to him and asked them to get a token for four samosas.

The cold climate made them want the samosas more. The samosas were flawlessly pyramid-shaped. The potato masala inside was neatly crumbed in a way that it was not too clumsy at the same time, not very hard. The potato masala contains potato(obviously), peas, chilly powder, garam masala and a pinch of salt. The wheat layer that surrounds the masala was medium-sized and not too crispy. They were served with a mint chutney which was a classy combination. The youngsters mouth watery; they slowly took one samosa dipped in that mint chutney and took a bite gently with a dripping chutney. As they chewed with their eyes closed, they felt the taste of every ingredient of the samosa. The boys felt chills in their spine as they swallowed.

"Aweeeee… dude… this is the best." said Karn.

"Yes!!!" said Aadi with a little droplet that filled his right eye.

Dive into the past

Quickly, they were immersed in a conversation about the new joinee ugly girl.

"Did you see that girl in the morning. She was very different. Don't know whether I will get along with her. I don't feel really connected."

"Yes Aadi, I saw. Hope we don't have any business with her."

"Certainly not eye to eye. Sorry, that was mean." laughed Aadi.

The teacher's voice was like a lullaby after lunch to all the students. The students woke up when they heard that the seating arrangements were to changed.

Aadi prayed to be seated near the beautiful girl; instead he was forced to sit near the new girl. Aadi was in a seat of awkwardness when the girl started talking. She smiled at him and introduced herself. He was not making any eye contact and introduced himself by seeing his fingernails.

"See. I am finding it difficult talking to you. Can we just sit and listen to the class," told Aadi in a husky voice.

The new girl just smiled, burying her hurtful feelings. At the same time, the weather was filled with tears from the cloud.

After school, the boys were cycling back to their house, talking about the day.

Dive into the past

"You are being a little rude to the new girl Aadi. Take it easy. She is also a human being," Karn politely said.

"It's just I don't feel like I want to talk to her. If Indira sat with me, I would feel free to talk to her. Because firstly, she is beautiful and second I have known hersince second grade."

"Well appearance isn't everything Aadi. Feel free."

"Lucky for you, I am the one who is gonna sit with her for the entire year." murmured Aadi.

"Sorry." Said Karn looking viciously at him.

"Ahh...I will try."

They have a routine of stopping by the lake and enjoying nature for a while. The lake was like a queen of all the lake put together. It had a tiara of lime colour grass and glitters of magenta pink flowers. There was a huge rock which they tried to move for years but couldn't like a diamond in the tiara. Its beauty was seized by the harsh weather. The drizzling climate forces them to leave without even taking a glance at the lakeview.

The next day, the students were informed to do a project forming a team with their bench mate. For the sake of marks, he broke his comfort zone by talking to the new girl.

"Look. To be frank, I am still uncomfortable talking to you but I guess this project will break the ice for me. Is that ok with you?" He ordered.

Dive into the past

The ugly girl shook her head involuntarily. A ray of sunlight passed through the window, glaring Aadi's eyes.

He suddenly woke up when the sunlight hit his eyes and found that the bus stood motionless because of the signal. Aadi heard the songs played by the vehicle horns and the shouting drivers who had been overtaken. The picture captured by eyes was warm. The smokes from the vehicle and hard-working beggars pretty much sums up the journey to their job for everyone in the city. Aadi just smiled at the moment and went back to sleep. Again, went to a dream state.

In the dreams, the following day.

Aadi and the new girl were discussing the project.

"Why are you always smiling? Do I look funny?" He asked doubtfully.

"No. If you write in your heart that everyday is the best day in the year then even you will be smiling now."

"Well good for you. Easy for you to say," said Aadi uncertainly.

Aadi and the new girl was planning to do a working model of the solar system from the perspective of earth.

"So, the thing you said yesterday is stuck in my head. It's actually made sense. Do you think today is a best day?" Aadi said in a friendly manner.

Dive into the past

"It's "TODAY". My favourite day." chuckled the new girl.

Aadi seems to find her interesting. The new girl was suddenly seen as an interesting girl in his eyes. They talked when the teacher was continuing her lecture.

"Ok, this is all of a sudden. Do you consider yourself ugly? You don't have to answer it. Sorry"

"Nobody is ugly. It's only people with different taste."

"If I call you ugly, would you accept it."

"I am a girl. I would gladly accept and smile."

"What do you mean by you're a girl?"

"Girls are defined as things that only accept and doesn't argue in this society. Soyou get the joke right," told the interesting girl with an embarrassed smile.

During lunch Aadi sat with Karn. Karn took Aadi's lunch and appreciated Aadi's mom for making that wonderful dish. Aadi disagreed by telling Karn'smom to deserve that appreciation. Friendships taught us sharing of food is not a sin and also that giving without any expectations is an actual thing. Karn told Aadi that the interesting girl had been taken half day leave. Aadi confessed to Karn that she is an out-of-the-box thinker, and he found it appealing.

Dive into the past

"Good to see you change." Said Karn smiling and eating Aadi's food.

Aadi sat alone on the bench, wondering what was the fascinating thing she was doing and was questioning what stories she would have told then.

"Where were you yesterday afternoon?"

"I was in hospital. I have a disease which I am surprisingly uncomfortable talking to you. Either way you were happy right because I wasn't there." She said with a smile.

"Ah...well yes...yes. And How can you smile when you tell this horrible news?"

"It's nothing I just wanna "live" rest of my life. So, what happen to the project?"

"You are living now and smiling doesn't make you live, it tells that you have lost your mind. Yes. Well why do you want to make it in Earth view?"

"Hmm...I am living in the moment. I read a book yesterday, it quoted "If you know when you're going to die, you will view the world differently." That really stuck me. Now why earth? you know we consider earth as mother of all lifeforms right and not the father. It's because women should be treated with respect similar to the respect that we give our earth. They continuously work for their home and don't get paid and are taken for granted just like earth. They are not allowed to follow what they pursue like the earth which only revolves

Dive into the past

around the sun. Ha Ha Ha. Funny right. I considered this project as a tribute to all the women out there."

"Wow. You are... different." Said Aadi astonished, and looked outside to notice a breezy blissful weather with very tiny droplets of rain hitting his face.

Suddenly the girl stopped talking and fainted. She was taken to the hospital. Aadi didn't realise what she quoted was literally the truth. He was mesmerised by what the girl told him and was thinking the whole afternoon. He then saw everything with a different mindset all of a sudden, the beautiful girl appeared as a girl and not an object. The crackling fan sound was like a music. The teacher's sweat felt like a stream of meaningful thoughts. The random writings on the bench made him blush. The whispering voice of his classmate about the power ranger was so fascinating. The football match played inside the classroom was more engaging than the real one. The blackboard looks pretty colourful to him. The smile of Karn was so warming to the seriously cold climate outside. A flash of his mom's smile came in front of his eyes. He realised that HE WAS "LIVING" HIS LIFE.

Then, that evening, the teacher came up with the news that Mariam was dead.

The school was finished, and tomorrow was declared a holiday due to her death. It started raining heavily. Aadi didn't wait for his friend. He

Dive into the past

was riding his cycle alone to the lake with a choking throat. His face was full of raindrops, with one hot drop dripping from his left eye.

"NO...NO..NO!! Do I have feeling for her? I dint feel any connection. I dint even consider her as a friend. OH GOD."

He sat on the rock. Slowly the clouds drifted away. The bright light of the sun hit the water. The unstable movement of water reflected the rays making it look like a cosmos in the ground. The sunset was red as Liverpool's jersey. The lime green grass was twinkling back the sunlight through the water droplets on them. Birds flew with complete freedom. A butterfly with a cut in one of its wings sat on his hand. He resonated the butterfly to Mariam and the weather with Mariam's emotion. The cold and unfriendly weather was her inner feelings, and now as the sun shines, she has found her freedom. The rock felt like his heart when she was still with him. He finds a crack in that unmovable rock which tells that his heart has also opened now.

"I am sorry. You're a pure soul and I missed a good friend. You taught being a girl and ugly shouldn't stop anyone." He cried to the butterfly.

The butterfly flew slowly towards the lake with utmost elegance. Aadi was widemouthed by the view.

"It is wonderf...."

Dive into the past

"Sir. We have reached the school sir. Get up."

Back to the reality.

"fulllll" said Aadi with tears dropping from his eyes. "Oh sorry."

As he got down, he called his daughter.

"Mariam. I have reached the school. Did you have your breakfast?"

 He walks in the hallway where he once studied as a student, now as a professor. Because he thought teaching the world for a lifetime that Mariam taught him in a short time would change the world a little.

- Gautham.

Dive into the past

The Maths Class

"Your twelfth classes will begin tomorrow," said Ms. Parimala, our Maths Teacher. Suddenly there was silence everywhere in the class. Some were getting heart attacks already. Others were totally frozen.

"Mam, it's just November. And haven't even finished our half-yearly exams." asked Mohan with a lot of confusion.

"Didn't your seniors tell you about this. This happens every year. You should have known this by now" MS. Parimala replied.

"But it usually begins by Jan Mam. This year they are starting a bit too early," said Hari in a calm tone.

"Last year thy were not able to cover some topics in Zoology at time it seems. So they are starting a bit quicker this time. All these are for your good only," she replied. It was 4.30 P.M, and the bell rang. "Thank you, students. I had a great time teaching you all," she said with a heavy heart. "We will miss you too mam," the students shouted with all the thoughts of missing her classes. Everyone packed their bags and departed home. On her way to the parking, Ms.Parimala could see a set of boys standing in the corridor. "Why are you boys standing here?" she inquired. "Mam we are waiting to see you Mam. We are going to miss your classes badly. We are upset that the classes have ended," said Hari.

"Hari, are you upset that my classes have ended or you are fearful that from tomorrow you will have to attend Pandian sir's class," she asked with a grin.

"It's a mixture of both, Mam," he replied.

Mr. Pandian is the Maths teacher for the 12th standard. He is just like the villains in Tamil movies who talk less with his mouth and more in his hands and stick. But still the most renowned teacher in the school, he has zero anger management. He is just like a scanner that has scanned the book from page 1 till the end. He had all the backing from the parents to beat the students, and he enjoyed such an opportunity.

"Don't worry about Sir. He is a gem of a person. You will come to know about him soon," she said. They had reached the bus parking, and everyone bid farewell to Mam and got onto their respective school buses fearing the worst.

The next day the timetable was published, and there was two maths class daily. There were four sections in the 12th standard—two sections of Bio-Maths and two sections of Maths-Computer. The biology group students were grouped into one for the maths classes alone. The first two periods of the day was maths class always.

"We should never open our mouth in the maths class," said Sibi. "We four can occupy the middle

Dive into the past

row. I have heard that he always asks questions to the people in the first and last row," he added. The other three nodded, and they rushed to get the middle bench in the middle row.

These four boys are the closest friends the school. They always sit, roam, and-play together. Hari is the one who gets good scores on all the tests. Sibi was the mischievous one. Mohan was the flirty one, and Mukilan was the funniest and the one who got caught by all the teachers. So both the class. There were two rows in front of the boys unoccupied. "If these two rows are not occupied quickly before he comes, he will call us to occupy the front rows," mukilan said fearfully. Mohan occupied the left most corner and Mukilan the right-most corner. Sibi sat to the left of Mohan, and Hari sat next to him. Mohan saw that a few girls were standing at the corner searching for a place. He signalled them that seats were available here. The girls rushed and occupied those benches.

"Maybe us having a combined class is actually good," Hari said to Mukilan." Why so," asked Mukilan with a confused face. Hari signalled him to look forward. Mukilan was not able to understand. "Dude, Anamika is sitting in front of us," he said, all blushing. She was sitting exactly in front of Hari.

"I noticed that long time back. If you try to talk with her and Dinesh see's that he will kill you. If Pandian see's you he will kill you. So please erase

Dive into the past

any thoughts of trying to talk to her and sit quietly," said Mukilan in a commanding tone.

"Okay!" Hari nodded. Mr. Pandian entered the class, and all students chorused a Good Morning. He signalled them to sit. He was the most unorthodox teacher of the school, who never tucks in the shirt, who never carries books to the class nor any test papers.

"Good morning students, I am Pandian your maths teacher. You might have heard about me from your seniors. There are two main things that you have to follow in my class, one is getting good marks. Good marks mean getting a pass mark. But the most important thing is discipline. That has the highest priority," he said, giving a brief about his methodology.

"So we will quickly move on to the class. I am going to start with Chapter 1, Functions and Unions. This an easy chapter and you will get at least three ten marks questions from this chapter" he started taking classes. As it was two hours, class all started getting tired after an hour. He could literally see na.

"Look I get that you all are tired after an hour of classes. So now you all can discuss the concepts within yourselves under one condition. I will ask a question about today's topic to an individual and if he answers it correctly, I will let you free for 15 minutes, or else I will start the next topic again.

Dive into the past

This will be followed in all my classes. So shall we start now" he asked.

"Yes, sir," some students chorused.

"Mukilan, stand up," he said. Mukilan stood up, trembling. "What is the formula to find A intersection B," he asked patiently as if he knew that Mukilan would not answer. And the exact thing happened that time. All the other three on the bench were laughing, holding their mouth. He again began taking classes.

"Can't you answer this?" Sibi asked Mukilan. He stared at him and said, "I am weak in maths and he knows that. He knows all the weak students in our class and will ask them questions, knowing that they will not answer."

That is his strategy. You could have told me. Or else Hari could have. What is he doing?" he asked Sibi.

"He is doing the most important job," said Sibi.

"That is?" asked Mukilan. "Looking at Anamika and blush like an idiot even though she is not looking at him." replied Sibi.

Mukilan called Hari and asked, "Didn't I ask you not to look at her in the beginning itself?". "Yes but I am going to see her daily. I will not talk to her. You know that I don't have that guts. So let me at least look at her. Please!" Hari replied. "Superb!!! Keep looking,"Mukilan replied with some sarcasm, and he added, "At least help me with the answers".

Dive into the past

"Ok, I will help next time," Hari replied.

At that same time Mohan had begun to speak with the girls in the front row. Sibicalled Hari and said "Mohan has started his work. He will surely speak to Anamika". Hari saw that Mohan had started talking to the girls in the front row. Mukilan also watched him and started laughing at Hari.

Days passed on, and months passed on. Still, the same things carried on. Hari did not talk to Anamika. Mohan had become her friend. But Hari's infatuation turned into a crush. And now the other three knew about this. Mohan urged him to talk to her. But still, Hari had a lot of hesitation.

But now the Maths period turned out to be the best period for all the students. Even though Mr. Pandian was short-tempered and would beat the students at times, he was the man who solved many of their problems and mainly helped them to go for P.T periods. He became jovial in the class, and hence all students enjoyed the class. Despite all these things, no student has answered his question. Mainly the question was asked in between five students, and Mukilan was one among them. He never answered the questions.

So, it was May. Holidays for all other students other than tenth and twelfth students. The duration of the maths period was increased to 3 hours. It was brutal torture for Mukilan but a breezy movie for Hari. But still, he had not talked to her. But one fine day Mr. Pandian was late for the class. That

Dive into the past

time, Anamika siting on the bench before turning back and asked Mukilan in a soft tone, "why don't you answer any question sir asks". Mukilan never expected such a question, and he stared at Hari. He then replied, "I actually do not like Maths. Pandian knows that and he targets me". She nodded as she said OK.

Then suddenly she turned towards Hari and said: "You can help him to answer the questions nah. You get good marks in all the tests. So you must listen the classes. If he tells the answer we will get a free period". Hari's heartbeat reached an all-time high. His heartbeat was so high that Mukilan could hear it. Sibi and Mohan were also watching that. Suddenly Mohan swopped in and said, "He knows the answers. But he never helps him". Hari was sweating a lot. His hands began to shake. With a lot of reluctance, Hari replied to her, "I am not a great listener. If I know the answer, I would help him."

"I also want a free period just as much you do," Hari said with a smile on his face.

"I see. But I have a doubt in yesterday's topic. I thought you would help me with that," she said.

"Which question?? I will try to solve that," Hari replied.

"Yesterday's topic. Integral Calculus. Do you know that?" she asked.

"I think I might know that," Hari replied.

Dive into the past

She pointed out the question and explained it to her in the best possible way.

"You are good teacher actually," she said.

"Not really. I actually knew the problem. That's why I was able to solve it," replied Hari with a gentle smile and shyness on his face.

At that moment, Pandian stepped in. He quickly went near the blackboard and wiped it clean, and started taking classes. While taking classes, Hari was still in dreamland and was shocked that Anamika had talked to him. On the other, he had a mild doubt whether Mohan had told anything about his crush to Anamika's friends. Immediately he called him and asked, "Did you tell her friends about my crush".

"Actually, I did not tell any one of them. But Roshini asked me whether you had some crush on Anamika. Someone has already told her it seems," he replied.

Hari was shocked by the fact that Anamika might know about his crush. But he did not have the guts to ask her about it. Days went on, but Anamika still went on asking doubts to him, which Hari wholeheartedly cleared all the time. They had become good friends in the meantime. So one fine day, during P.T period, the boys were playing cricket. At that time, Sibi, the best batsman in the school, hit the ball to the boundary. The ball kept on rolling to the shuttle court where girls were

Dive into the past

playing shuttle. He could see Anamika sitting alone. He picked the ball and threw it back, and walked towards her.

"Hey!! Why are you sitting here , alone??" he asked her.

"Nothing! Just thought that I would be alone for a while," she replied in a low voice such that even a small child would guess that she was upset about something.

"You are clearly not ok. If you have to talk about anything I am here always," he comforted her.

"Actually, I do have a problem. Promise me that you won't tell this to anyone else," she asked, stretching her hands to get a promise. Hari promised her that he would not say anything to anyone.

"I actually have a crush on someone in our college and I don't want to feel about him in such a way, but sometimes it seems impossible. I want to get rid of all these and concentrate on my studies. But I find it difficult sometimes," she said with some reluctance and some blush.

"Whom do you have a crush on?" asked Hari.

"That is a secret. Can you please help me here?? Please!" she pleaded.

"Atleast tell me which section he is" hair asked with anxiety.

Dive into the past

"He is from C section," she replied. All of Hari's dreams were shattered. He remained silent for a few seconds and replied stumbling, "Crushes are normal in this age. There is nothing to worry about. Just go with the flow. You will get past this stage quite easily. Don't worry about those and go and enjoy you're P.T period. We get those only once in a month," he replied, hiding all his pain.

"But he has become an addiction recently. I am not able to get over him," she added, rubbing salts to his wounds.

"You will get over him. Just remain calm when he is around you and just remember our twelfth examination and the sacrifices made by our parents to enable us good education. So you can get over these. If you had already talked to him, keep in mind that he is your friend and nothing more. Do you get me?" he advised himself, advising her.

"Ok. I get that. I will try to avoid those and thanks for your help as usual," she replied with a bright smile.

"Always, welcome," he replied with a fake smile. She then went to the tennis court and started playing, and Hari returned to cricket, and on reaching there, he broke the promise told about this to his friends. They advised him to move on. And he knew that was the only option. So he cleared his mind and told his brain that she was only his friend. He also knew that she would ask doubts to

Dive into the past

him, and at that time, he should let the emotion get the better of him.

Days passed on. At first, Hari found it hard to accept the reality, but then he slowly moved on. But he still enjoyed maths class the fun it used to bring in. He still used to clear Anamika's doubts, but he had the clarity that she was her friend and nothing more.

It was July 31. All the staff had completed the portions except Mr. Pandian. Maths period was the last period of the day, and he had just two sums left. He quickly finished the sums. Then he said, "Your portions are over. From Monday you will be given continuous tests. This is all for your good". People were not feared of the tests. But not attending Maths class was the most difficult one. Especially, Hari was distraught that he may never be able to speak to Anamika even as a friend thereafter. He knew that during revision, Girls would be in one room and boys would be in another room to study. So speaking with her will be literally impossible. He became silent, thinking about all those stuff. Suddenly, Anamika turned and said, "I will miss these talks between us. Those small talks were actually one of the best in this class for me."

Hari was totally moved, and controlling all his emotions, he replied, "Me too. These talks were the best actually."

Dive into the past

The bell rang, and officially the chances of him speaking to her nearly dropped to zero. Both exchanged byes and left home.

Then all the things Hari thought would happen had happened. He had a little chance of talking to her. But the one positive thing is that he spent all the time with the other three. Months passed on. They studied hard for the public exams. Dates were announced. They prepared hard and gave their best in all the exams.

On March 31, their schooling ended officially. Tears flooded among the four like a river. They had become so close by the passing of time. Even though everyone lived close to each other, they knew that this time would never come back. They got on the college bus and talked endlessly about staying in touch. Everyone had gotten off the bus, and Hari was the last one on the bus. His stop also arrived, and he got down and reached home with a heavy heart of missing his friends. He opened his bag and took the question paper out, and kept it in a file for future reference. But he could find another paper in his bag. He took it out. It was a letter. There was no mention of the writer of the letter. Hari began to read the letter

"TO: Hari Prakaash R S

Thank you for all the moments. The moments I shared with you will be the best in my life. You will always be an important person in my life. You are one of the main reasons because of whom I will get

Dive into the past

good marks in Maths. I never had a crush on anyone from C class. It was always from the one from A1. The one who sat right behind me. The one whom I tried to talk with daily. And the one who advised me to get over it. It has always been you. I did not express it earlier because I knew that you had a crush on me. We had to study well and get good grades and get into a good college, and I hope we will do that. So now, as school is over, I have the courage to express this. I will call you once I get a new mobile phone. Your friends also knew about this. They helped me a lot at times. They gave me this idea. You are the luckiest to have such friends and, of course, me. I am looking forward to meeting you again."

Hari had tears of joy. So it was not the end of the journey. It was the beginning of an incredible journey that will last a lifetime. He considered himself as the luckiest man to have such friends and such a girl in his life.

Every Hari in this world deserves such friends and a Anamika. I am not sure whether everyone has a girl like Anamika from their schooling, but surely they will have friends like these who care about us without expectations.

Lucky are those whom still are in contact with their school friends and still have them as their best friends

Hari Prakaash

Dive into the past

The Untaught Education

It was an evening around 6 pm at my Periyamma's house; I was in 9th grade, I had to do an assignment and submit for the schoolwork. It was the year 2015 where the internet was not as affordable as of today, there used to be only one smartphone per house maximum, and internet for a month was limited to 1 Gb, so we had to use stingily the net in order to make sure we had internet for the whole month. Generally, we should keep it under 2G network for minimal usage of the net, which we used only for WhatsApp and for school project work and rarely we would use youtube to see any trolls, trailers etc. Still, at that time, I finished the entire quota; I had to do an assignment where we copy-paste from a website to a word document, attach some pictures, print and submit. It would get us 4 or 5 out of 10 marks which were enough to pass the assignment. So, I was begging my mom for Rs.50, "Ma, Please, I am sorry that I finished up the quota watching youtube, but I need the money now to go to net center and finish up the assignment, I need to submit the printouttomorrow". The smart students usually write the entire assignment and would get good marks. Students like me would do just the copy-paste and submit as a plagiarised assignment and get minimal marks. After a long struggle and scolding frommy mom and Periyamma. I got the Rs.50 and ran to the net

Dive into the past

centre. I got the computer in the middle cubicle, and my work was just 15 min, copy-pasting the information, adding pictures, saving and printing. Once it's done, I go to the chrome and type on the search bar 'xvideos.com'. And then immediately, my whole body starts warming up, my brain starts secreting more dopamine with just a click away. My brain would start scanning for the videos that are the best to watch with the remaining time left, as if like a wildfire. I would keep on watching videos after videos till the remaining time is left. The net centre would have drapes for every cubicle after everything is done. I would take the printout, pay and leave. Previously when I mentioned I would use up the limited internet on the phone watching youtube, it was only partly true; most of the data was streamlined to Porn.

Time to give a little background about my school, after 6thgrade, the boys and girls were not allowed to sit on the same bench, it's divided as two rows for girls and two rows for boys. There existed an invisible rule that boys and girls shouldn't talk with each other and should talk only if were necessary. It was believed among guys who doesn't talk with girls and have many guy friends was really cool. The teachers didn't teach any sex education; they announced it as self-learning chapters. The school didn't teach properly about women's menstruation cycle to boys; it was just a five-mark question, according to them. The school didn't teach us what

Dive into the past

kind of mental state and physical pain they would be in at that time. The school didn't teach us how a man should see a woman in society. The school didn't teach us how to talk to a girl, how to be gentle with the opposite sex, how to make love to a woman, how to not treat them as just a mere property. It didn't teach us that we should not judge the opposite sex and abuse them. As a result, the students had unwanted fantasies about sex, and they sought sex education through porn. As a result, they didn't have proper knowledge about anything opened the door wide open into the male chauvinist society, which led to consequences like students would immediately label a guy and girl as couples if they talk more than what is 'necessary' or if they laugh together while speaking to each other. Girls will be slut-shamed if she talks to guys often. But I had only a few friends, and I didn't go with the opinion of teasing women if they spoke with boys beyond what was necessary. As for my story, my mind mostly dwelled in porn, whereas outside, I acted as if I was disgust watching porn and exhibited myself as a decent guy among friends. I wasn't open to my friends in this particular topic.

The habit of watching porn made me insecure about my Penis size. I started believing myself the size of that part matters a lot. The huge size the opposite sex will be more satisfied during intercourse was my belief. This thought made me really petrified that no girl would love me or I wouldn't be able to satisfy my partner in future. So not having any

Dive into the past

knowledge, I started measuring it and believed stroking it would enlarge it, and accidentally, I found it ejaculates semen. I was in a perplexed state without knowing to whom should I share my doubt about what I had done. Thus, I shared with one of my closest friends, Santhosh. He explained to me that it's normal, and he revealed he also does that while watching porn, but I was not sure if that was healthy and whether it would cause any side effects. Then I consulted one of my cousins, Nirmal, who is two years elder to me. He was laughing at my doubts and made me feel frightened that it would reduce the bone strength making it brittle, and would shorten my lifespan, and it would make my spine weak and advised me to keep it only once a month if I felt uncontrollable. But as days passed, I became addicted to porn and Masturbation. I generally felt uninterested in any work I would start, and my mind would deviate from watching porn and masturbating. After every time I masturbated, immediately I felt guilty about myself for no reason. I stopped participating in any competitions in schools became lonelier, and a thirst to win in any challenging interschool sports or talent competitions. I started getting low marks in my subjects, and my average fell to 70%. Eventually, I started hating myself for not achieving anything much in life. Even though I knew that my porn addiction was the cause of my downfall, I couldn't come out of it. I stopped setting a goal and achieving it.

Dive into the past

Thus, as the days passed, I was just an average lonely student `indifferent in academics and extracurricular activities. I took an average mark in the 10th standard and took the 3rd group, thinking there wouldn't be much to study. During 11th, I had a friend named Sona. We studied in the same class from LKG to 5th grade. After five years, we were back again in the same class. She is a voracious reader of novels and literature. Once I noticed she was reading 'Half Girl Friend' book by Chetan Bhagat. Knowing that his books are romantic and have a lot of sexual relationships among male-female characters, I gathered my courage and asked her if she could lend me that book after she completed it. She smiled slightly and said she would lend me Revolution 2020 for now as she has completed it. That book changed my opinion on love. Initially, I was reading the book for the romance and sex scenes. But in the end, I cried. While returning the book to her, I told her the book changed my opinion on love; women mentioned that I cried at the end. She smiled and said she also cried. That day evening, I received a Fb request from her, we started talking a lot about the book, and she was introduced to many other books. She told me to read author Kalki books and to start with Sivagamiyin Sabatham and Ponniyin Selvan, which I remembered my mother had in our home. So I started reading Sivagamiyin Sabadham. I fell in love with the book that I forgot porn or masturbating and listening in the class. She once saw that I was reading the bookkeeping under the

Dive into the past

desk in Commerce class and laughed at my situation. She would constantly ask where I was in the story and would chat endlessly about the characters. Gradually I started reading books which she suggested because I liked her, and while speaking with her, I was so happy more than anything. She had BSNL landline, which was free of charge if we spoke between 9 pm to 9 am, for which we used to get up at 4 am every morning to speak on the phone while our families were asleep. During the mid 11th standard, she proposed to me on a fine evening on Phone. She said," I feel something more about our relationship. Do you feel the same?". I smiled to myself and said Yes. Eventually, we fell in love and started talking more about intimate subjects about our sexual desires. When she began to understand my view on sex, she found that I watch Porn. I was a bit afraid and thought she would think of me as a pervert and break up with me. She then told me she also watched porn sometimes. Initially, I was shocked; till then, I never imagined in my life that women would watch porn. Then she made me understand that women too have sexual desires in them. She then while conversing, made me to realise that Sex is more like connection of hearts than just connection of the body. She reads a lot of literature books and would explain to me the characters about how a guy should approach his partner before Sex. She made me understand that in Sex the women at first would need to Trust and believe completely their partner without any fear and should engage

Dive into the past

in foreplay before the intercourse in order to set the mood to achieve orgasm. If their partner is not in that mood, we should not force them, which would break the trust. Till then, I didn't know the words what orgasm or foreplay meant. She then realised that I have poor knowledge of sex and taught me about the female body about their sexual parts, their menstrual cycle, how would their mood swing during periods. She made to understand why women use Sanitary napkins and how much pain they would feel in their abdomen during the period. This made me realise that sex education is not in watching porn. In a nutshell, she made me understand that sex is a bigger subject than Chemistry or physics or mathematics, and it's an everyday learning process. But this society and religion make it taboo unnecessarily. If society would just tell the truth as it is, people would not have any fake fantasies and would not treat their opposite gender as an object and constantly put them into abuse.

I was so angry with myself for being a fool till that part in my life; she calmed and said, let us be the change we wish to see in society and will be a better parent in the society. Eventually, she changed my thought process and made me concentrate on my studies and made me realise that we need to become self-sufficient and independent in future to marry each other and start a family.

-Surya

Dive into the past

The Unsettled Yearning

The Black& White combo of "Board & Chalk impression" speaks it all!!

The lessons of life, gifted friendship, hardly science & its related topics, accompanied in life, from school. The mind keeps wandering in the school every time, rewinding the Lively life as a student, moving to the classrooms and the places allotted to sit, the corridor wandered with friends, the angels-taught selfless love, called teachers. That sacred place got its special vibration in the living hearts of old students. Taken to the land of experiences by teachers, many lessons commenced to grasp.

All it started, with the unplanted seedlings, brought with loudest heartbeats, quivered sobs over the odd environment. Fortunately, its culmination happened earlier. The separation of the lively, active little birds, which were all chirping together.

Recollecting Life as a sturdy student initially comes the fear of failing uniformity and punctuality, Unchanged respectable responses towards staffs, yet maintaining a classroom that quarrels forever. The hustle-bustle morning preparation. Facing the exam seasons with complete preparation, still

Dive into the past

premises over doubts. The angels of school express complete love and care in her own way of punishments and monotonous pieces of advice.

And the immature friendship adventitiously blossomed, stick with the Gangs of likely minds. With uncommon minds, inside one room, "The great classmates!" Grown together year by year under the same roof & before the very same blackboard. Unsaid assignments allotted, Secret roles to play!! The last hour teacher before exams, the class leader evolved to be a Judge, solving the silly fights, the entertainer being the class's favourite, the crazy conversations made the school days complete. Respected according to the unique roles acted every day, found nowhere outside the school. We worked together giggling, especially complaining over extra classes and additional homework, it includes!

The painful times arouse after school life, the school student forcefully transformed into a citizen, weighed with many responsibilities. It was no more a sapling; it was watered and ventilated perfectly, grown a giant tree. Not a playful school student anymore with uniforms.

And life goes on, with the carrier started in school. Even though, craving to be the same student again, to march towards that exact classroom. It was just a

Dive into the past

failed dream, submerged within us, the constant reminder of school and its life. Don't worry about the missing pieces of "Jigsaw puzzle life." It is not stolen but kept hidden in the school as ardent memories.

As a student failed to sense the millions of love and care that the school showered. It seems to be a concluded school story, but it's an unfinished love story that keeps living within!

"Life of Being a student is regretted; only after losing the identity as a student!"

- Shri Logitha.

Dive into the past

Why do Farewell betide???

In everyone's lifetime, there will be most memorable and unforgettable journeys that were much secure and close to heart, and that cannot be erased away from their memory. Conducive to that, one's school life journey will be the most secured feeling in the heart it will be connected with the soul. It will be turned into the soulful memory of one as like that last bench atrocities, uncompleted diary works, copying homework in a rush during the morning, computer class atrocities, laboratories jovial moments and sad moments of PT period occupied by the Maths teacher are never gained treasured golden memories. Every year starting day of school we all go with new uniforms, new Tiffin box, new bag, new lunch bag, new eraser, pencil, pen these all we will be showing to our peer group that was the happiest thing in our school life and the most important thing we all will be expected to get a good friendly class teacher, those moments are like a husband stands out in the delivery ward with the expectation of a boy or a girl child. When the teacher arrives, we all know to sing a song that is "Gggooodddddddmmornnninggggggg maaaammmmmm," though we didn't go to the music class, we all know to sing this song perfectly with the rhythm and chorus. The class teacher will be sweet and friendly in the first class. Their first intention is to select the representative of the class. At that time, we didn't know about their plan, but sorrowfully the representative work was to spy on us, and secretly

Dive into the past

he or she would be the pet of the class teacher in primary class. We all think the post of the representative is honoured position like a president we all expect to become a monitor of the class and we think that this is a prestigious job but in the second class we come to know that the representative is completely a help worker to the class in charge and he or she is the most pitiful mate in our school life as we all make him or her as a puppet to us and for our mistakes too he or she will get great scolding from every teacher who comes to our class. Every subject teacher compares us with the nearby class that they are too good and very obedient to him or her. Still, the reality is to that compare class, he or she will be saying that our class is obedient and good when compared to them, so this was the tricked by the teachers, and they still don't know that we had a friend in that class and we discuss this.

Then comes our silent killer friend. The whole day before the exam, he or she will be with us, and when we asked have you studied for the exam? He or she will say nothing he or she studied and don't know about anything, but when the paper comes, he or she will be the second topper of the class that was the great betrayal moment in the school life. Then who didn't show the answer script in the exam hall was the stone-hearted person in the class we all scold him or her whenever we see them in our school life. We all listen to the class carefully when the teacher explains their own life matters and overcome struggles, etc., then the teacher teaches the lesson. When our best friend is absent from the school, the whole class looks like a desert to us, but when we're absent, the day will have two PT periods, one

Dive into the past

teacher will be absent, and the next day when we come to our class, our bosom mates explains with a happy face all the well-wished things happen to him or she is the most tragic moment in everyone's life.

We all have a classmate who always argues with the teacher, and sometimes a great battle goes between them; that time we all will be in heaven we all enjoy the fight with great happiness, through the fight the whole period is gonna over we expect the most.

We all spend time together with our best friends every day in the class; each second we will be with them than with our family we spend time in the school for about 8 hours. Friendship is a great treasure we acquire in school than knowledge. The school taught us many necessary things: how to share, live in this society, and live independently. The teacher teaches a lesson for about three to four hours that time we can't understand that but the best teaching aid for us is our friend who teaches us the whole lesson before the 10 minutes of examination, choosing a friend is the most important thing in our school life, and that builds our character.

In these more jovial moments are present in our school life, but the most heartful and cheerful timing in school life is the lunch period—one tiffin box with a favourite dish. Every hand inside and it get a finish.

Our mum's cooking gets bored. Other peer-group moms cooking we adore. After the bell rang, it was the lunch break though the teacher continued the lesson heart shakes. We all tried to escape. That was the most playful timing than the PT period with the girls' gang giggles and gossips; boys' gang pen fights,

Dive into the past

and some play handi cricket — those were evergreens. Years passed, exams passed, we all enjoyed about 14 years of school life with morning tuitions, evening tuitions, everything studied over, but those went like a jet in the sky. One day arrived with the name called "Farrwell" then only we could realise we are grown up, and it was the end of our school life, and we had certain responsibilities the most fearful one It was a heartbreaking moment to everyone that takes some time to understand. Sometimes we waste the most fruitful thing in school life, which is ripened with great taste, and now we can realise those mistakes. That was the period where every clay changed into a great statue. Until the last breath, everyone will remember these happiest days and are the days with no responsibilities, no feelings, and nothing only to have fun and enjoyments and still now I feel why do the Farewell arrives as soon and take away those happiest days from us and I weeps for the past

Why do "FAREWELL" betide???

- Saranika.

Dive into the past

Tranquillised in time

As leaves pursued the trail of the cool breeze
and heavenly scent of the peach blossoms adorned
the air;
bolting me in the vault of time,
my heavy eyelids
stole a caress,
while Paganini flaunted
his violin strings.

I saw myself, dainty as rose,
flying planes and dressing up dolls.
Carefree, cheerful,
relishing candies and lollies,
towering in oversized red heels,
desperately convincing mother about the sheer
perfection.

And one summer morning,
she entered that room, reluctant.
Scattered Barbies and unicorns ,
screaming kids and beaming eyes.
Lost tack of time,
I saw her running happily to that room ,until,
multiplication tables and exams
haunted her dreams.
Teary palms and quivering lips,
first speech was a disaster indeed.

Dive into the past

Fake signatures and
dramatic excuses for
the flawed punctuality.
Spent nights drooling over vampires and
werewolves
while relation with trigonometry
continued to be a monologue.
Tension and stress smirked maliciously,
board exams awoke the monk in her.
Neighbours she never had rolled her dice
chanting fake mantras.
But triumphant, she stuffed their curious mouths
withdelicacies .
Sky was unusually blue and
the sun gleamed mysteriously.
Shattered mirror,
mother wiping tears in the attic,
and she knew,
life would never be the same.
With echoes of endless complaints
she was in Tartarus;
lost in the wailings below,
with no dreams ,no hope .
Schooling was just a ritual,
words and numbers
made no sense,
friendship was a hoax.
Sick and tired of searching,
happiness was long lost.

Cleaned up the shattered vase ,

Dive into the past

served drinks to the old man's guest
on the empty armchair,
while girls grooved to the melody of cupid.
Ramblings of class mates grew unbearable,
eyes bored into hers,
with pity.
But no-one cared,
they just stared,
and kept on staring;
while she was trying hard,
not to let the tears roll.
Dragged into all family battles,
her twisted family stood bashfully,
ruining her life.
Only if she'd said 'No',
only if she'd asked her creator to solve her own
problems,
only if she'd spent the nights learning instead of
wiping tears,
only if she didn't care,
she wouldn't be so broken now.

Realised happiness is not -
blue diamonds or pearls,
cars or exquisite curves.
It's the simple courage-
to say NO,
to accept your flaws,
to understand you have one life,

should we spend it wiping others tears

Dive into the past

when we are already drowning in ours?
Jolt of this intricacy,
opened my eyes to the glorious sunset.
I stood in awe to these words,
"When its time to sow your seeds,
Don't waste time plucking others weeds",
hypnotised.

-   Sandra.

Dive into the past

Abitha

The wonderful morning, hearing the sparrow chirping, the cool wind, astonishing sun, and the chattering sound!!! The joyful times in our school.

School is the most awesome phase of our childhood. When we say school, what are the things which struck a chord, first and foremost, friends, then the scolding's that we got for our friend's mistake, the lies we told our teachers, and importantly the blackboard.

A child begins their life at school, where the blackboard makes the future bright. School brings out their abilities and trains them to face a new world.

Moreover, students are the future of a nation and going to be the policymakers. Thus the blackboard has an indirect influence on the nation's literacy & nation's development.

In 2020, the literacy rate in developed countries like Japan, Australia, and America was 99.9%, whereas in undeveloped countries like Afghanistan, Iraq, and Pakistan are about 60%. Thus it is evident that a country with a high literacy rate has good policymakers, and they are the innate gift for the nation's development. On the other hand, illiteracy is not a misfortune, but it is not an advantage all the while.

Literacy builds self-esteem and overall quality of life. Literacy is the only methodology to beat poverty. If you do not have the basic literacy skills, you will never have the quality of life you are looking for or deserve.

As per studies, it is proved that for a country's growth the education is the most important thing. In undeveloped countries, the crime rate increases, and the illiteracy of a country affects internationally because the illiterates turn into terrorists and don't let others educate. Nobel laureate Ms. Mallala Yousafzai struggled for the same cause. She fought against the Tehrik-e-Taliban Pakistan's (TTP's) restrictions on education for girls.

A country that does not face the blackboard will not face the light.

"If you concentrate on the blackboard, your name will be on the leader board, otherwise underscored"
Ms. Abitha Sivaraman

Dive into the past

Don't you know me by now

Stopped loving you.
Not in any way, I
Would say; once more!
Lets heat up the spark
Hatred I was filled,
Because I was blinded by the
Lights of our love.
And I only remember
The times we didn't have
And I don't want to think about
Your puppy eyes and happy face,
Hobbit ears and sad tears
I'll forget you
I could never utter,
You stayed in my head beneath all the clutter
But no,
My mind; was a blackboard
I erased you from
I wish,
I wasn't numb.
It was a daydream delusion
Not as if,
You and I were in fusion.
(Now read from bottom to top)

Nagapranith.

Dive into the past

Symbol

Sir, this is the busiest avenue in this country. You'll see everything that this country has to offer here," said the guide, looking at his patron...who was already lost amidst the revving cars of the highway, blinding lights of the market place and the unnerving feeling of being a man of colour for the first time in his life.

"Yeah... your country looks so lively in the night! I mean look at them....even the walls are full of graffiti", responded the tourist.

"But I'm seeing repeated black patterns on the walls all over the city," he added.

"That sir, is the black board! Its a symbol," said the guide

"What? the symbol that all the graffiti artists in the city are copy cats?" he smirked. The guide smiled at him and did not say a word.

Later in the misty dark night away from the bustling streets, he settled down in his hotel after a busy day walking and seeing the country. He invited his guide for dinner that day and noticed that he was visibly in unrest but denied anything when asked. The guide was a relatively silent man for a guide. Well dressed and had deep roots among the natives of the country, and also had a way of expressing his country's history to the onlookers that made him stand out.

"I'll take white," he said, after convincing his ever silent tour escort to a game of chess. When asked

Dive into the past

why, he replied by saying, "It suits my colour and most importantly it moves first."

"Ofcourse," said the guide.

"Pawn to E4", white made the 1st move... a classic white opening move as any 'chessy brain' would know...

"Pawn to C5", the guide came up with the best black opening move straight outta the books of the Sicilian defence... the game went on... the tourist slowly slaughtered the pawns......he took down the knights... eliminated both of the bishops, before 'checking the king. The guide had to sacrifice his queen to live to fight another battle, but the black king stood tall as if he had nothing to lose. He didn't move a square until the equation came down to the king, his ever-loyal pawn, and the manifestation of his strength, his rooks against an army of whities.

"Surrender, you know its a loosing battle," said the tourist...but before he could realise... he was losing his cavalry and losing them quick... he tried escaping the late onslaught...but it was as if the board was working against him... as if the board had faded to black...in the end, all he could do...was to acknowledge the black king as it turned out to be a stalemate...

"Your king didn't even move a square!" He exclaimed to his guide after the game...

"Yes sir, he didn't... he stood his ground...even when the enemy army had a far better arsenal...even when his land was wet from the blood of his brothers...even when he lost his beloved queen...even when all hope seemed to be lost......he didn't give in....he died standing his ground for his

Dive into the past

people but lives in our hearts as a symbol..", said the guide.
 "The blackboard?" he asked...picking up the scent of a martyr from the guide's cryptic monologue...
 "Yes, sir, the blackboard,
 A symbol of resistance to any invader
 A symbol of hope and pride to every soul that calls this land home!".

- Nagapranith.

Dive into the past

Tomorrow

"I tried to make everything as pleasant and quick as possible....i hope the scene doesn't burn on you...I don't want to leave trauma and hurt...i cant put the burden of me on anyone else anymore...I know how blessed parts of my life has been...but i know im not good enough...I know it gets better, but I cant last that long...i dont want to die but sometimes i wish i was never born... don't hate me please...i don't know what else to do...goodbye", he read it again, sitting in the corner of a bustling street beside some people standing in a queue, while a tiny teardrop crossed his overgrown stubble and fell on the paper, as if it was a full stop to this letter and hence to all his suffering. The lights were flickering everywhere so much...he could barely keep his eye open, the horns were as loud as pòssible, and they kept on coming...there was no escape from the constant chaos in the street...enough to drive anyone crazy.

He looked at the letter...smiling at the fact that this was going to be the last sonnet he ever wrote.... 'smiling lips, teary eyes and a treacherous soul' was the story of his life.

"What if I disappear...nothing changes...life just passes", he said to himself.

"Free passes......free passes, the show's going to begin..." he heard a man yelling at the front of the building next to him...he stood up...took one of them...but when he opened the door to enter the show....he was confused..., "why did i do that?", as he did nothing of it intentionally....but he got in anyway

Dive into the past

and found a seat in a dark corner so that no one would see him cry.

Knives, pills, ropes...things kept flashing in his head...thinking about how his end was going to be....but suddenly, the music hit...the screen opened, the shenanigans began...

Came out a man, 'the magician,' with a serious face and hid himself in a cloak as if it was to protect the audience from the darkness within him.

First he made a pigeon to fly...out of thin air, then went on to take a rabbit out of the hat....he even did the sword thing with his assistant....everyone knew everything was just a trick or an illusion and the tools were fake.....and even the graceful magician knew that he aint no Albus Dumbledore....but people were so into the act......they chose to ignore what they knew to be true." Isn't that how we get by....forget what we know to be true!", he said to himself.......this train of thought was interrupted by ," And for the main event.....i present you the Blackboard!", said the magician, it was not even a board...it was a box, but the wandless wizard had a charm on the audience, that they couldn't get out of...so he continued," Long lived a man, who captured angels and demons and imparted them into this vessel.....far great soldiers and warriors have fell facing the wrath of the forbidden souls and no man alive knows the fate of the fallen, for they would've been vanished in a blink of an eye". Chills passed down the audience as the magician asked for a volunteer expecting no one would...but he did...he reached the stage and stood before the fear struck faces of the masses.....the magician whispered to him, "relax its just a trick and don't forget to stay

Dive into the past

silent," and helped him get into the blackboard, before closing the board the magician said," There's always a way out!", and suddenly, "ABRACADABRA," he falls into a trap door under the box and hence, the sorcery.

He fell into a small cabin, dark and tight it was.... suddenly it was as if the world had stopped moving, it was the physical manifestation of how he felt every single day, every single minute in the night when he couldn't close his eyes. He was motionless as if he was dead, until the moment...he listened to the screams, the gasps of breath taken, and the awe of the audience filled with the aura of the presentation......he was in a chamber under the stage when suddenly it hit him....

"I disappeared.....and it mattered!?" he exclaimed in disbelief......" I mean people cared about a person who they barely knew?" There aroused a need....not a need to die, but a dying need to feel free. He finally broke free of the enclosure, wiggling through a path that leads to the outside...both in mind and body...suddenly he realised that the lights weren't too bright, but he was in a dark place...He uttered the words which would drive him ever since, "I may not be good enough....but I cant live my entire life proving that I am."

He needed to disappear to find himself....he needed that moment of anonymity in the dark, cramped chamber to know that he could break free. He needed that blackboard to realize that even on your worst day... there's always a tomorrow !!

-   Nagapranith.

Dive into the past

Remembering The Initial Steps Of My Teenage Education

Bright, colorful, vivid, and beautiful it was. Can we frame it this way, "life was simpler when we learnt from the blackboard." The blackboard is superior to all the smart boards we have ever come up with.

The blackboard meant different to all of us. Some of us never wanted our names to be written on it, some of us fought to erase what the teacher had previously written on it, some of us wrote thought for the day, numbers of students present and absent, total, date, etc. on it, some of us were amazing artists to draw on them, some of his wrote our own names and friends name on the board when no one was around and ran away, some of his players with the white chalk dust that resided and put it on our friends, some of us wrote our names with our crushes and runaway, etc., etc.

So Ironic and beautiful it is how a dark-colored board can just flash so many memories inside our minds and hearts. The blackboard got improvised to the whiteboard, to a smartboard, and now to our mobile or laptop screens. Blackboard is not an object. It was an era—one of the happiest and wondrous periods of our lives. The memories are colorful, where we all, without doubt, want to relive just once, where we all witnessed the beauty of life together. We all can be called too emotional if we imagine ten years from now revisiting our old school, same old class, grazing our fingers on the dirty blackboard, glazing our fingertips with chalk powder. We tend to tear up and

Dive into the past

get gushed up with different sweeps of memories and feelings.
It was such an unappreciated time of our life. So Vivid, so beautiful, so colorful.
Hey blackboard, we truly miss you.

-   Anjana Ravi

Dive into the past

Down The Memory Lane

This is not just a story to cross by. Though I have finished my schooling a long time ago, I still wish to go back to my childhood. I believe it is not only me but everyone's dream or at least a wish to be back to our childhood days. I wish to go back in memory lane to my school days every time I cross my school. It is the only place where we get everything. It is not just a place for education. It is where we find friends who will do anything to make us happy if we are sad. At that age, we don't know what caste is. We just know the only difference is boy and girl. This place has never failed to amaze me. I got my lifetime friendship here. If there is a problem for me, everyone will be there to give a solution; some will be quite funny, like even puncturing the teacher's two-wheeler, which we never tried but laughed aloud. The infatuation and crush start there without even knowing what even the thing is, thinking that it is the love of our life and daydreaming along with the classes which make many outstanding students in class. I still find it the funniest thing in my life. Rubbing the board clean for our favorite teachers, a daily new story for not finishing home work also followed by copying wrong answered homework with utmost confidence.

The first benchers getting covered with chalk dust during board cleaning. The slowest history period

Dive into the past

and short P.E periods all are never enough. While these are leisure memories, there are some tense situations like fighting for the corner seat in benches during class tests and hiding below the desks when teachers ask questions—getting our friends to stand up for the same. Bunking class by volunteering in extra curriculum. The highest competition is getting to go with our friend on distributing chocolates to the whole school. The most enjoyed one is the school anniversary cultural preparation which gives more class bunking and a lot more memories. Small fights between friends which never lasted more than two periods, copying during exams all last day ink fights and water rush are still dream end of every year we feel relieved as the term is over cursing school all along. Still, we always hope to go back there now as we are so happy only in that place. Every year at the end of exams everyone will spend the day we are going to other school hating this to the core. Still, every year we stayed in the same school, realizing that it is the best ever thing happened school is not just a place it holds emotions and memories together throughout life. I wish if I could just live even one day again in there. I'm sharing this in the belief that everyone will be feeling the same in their childhood. There are some children for whom the school is still a dream, but we all are blessed with this, so spread love and help someone to study, which I believe is the best to do in a human's life.

\-   Ram Mohan

Dive into the past

One Last Time

As the sunlight filtered in long transparent dusty tubes through the broken window glasses, the rusty walls lit up in a pale early morning glow. The shadows crept back into the creeks and corners of the shattered furniture. Spiders began to spin their endless cobwebs, and everything else was disturbingly still and lifeless. The air was damp, and the whole place smelled like the carpeted floor was rotting away.

A car approached the driveway of the house. It was Sarah's old Mercedes. Its been a couple of decades since they have moved to South Dakota. Her dad opened a new restaurant there, and they all had to move, which meant she had to change school again. She slowly opened the front door of the building, and it swung open in an eery creaking noise. As she set foot inside the house, a million memories came gushing to her mind like waves hitting the shore with all their might. She kept her hands to herself, cautious not to touch the thick mat of dust that had settled on top of all the things. She slowly went up the stairs to her room. The wallpapers were crumbling down. She went to the old mirror mounted on top of a vintage cabinet. It has come with the house from their previous owner. This victorian cabinet was something Sara was very adamant about taking to South Dakota with them,

Dive into the past

but her dad refused to do it anyways. She was admiring the beauty of the cabinet and suddenly remembered something. She tried to open the top left drawer of the cabinet, which she could open with a little struggle. The beautiful album was still there, where she last saw it. If only her father hadn't rushed the move, she would have taken this beautiful photo album with her. It was somewhere in between an album and a scrapbook. Sarah's dad had a Polaroid camera, and he religiously took a photo of her on every first day of school. She had made a collection out of those photographs and made a scrapbook out of it. She remembered even stealing the camera once to take it to school. She took the fragile album and sat on the floor. Suddenly the dust didn't matter to her. She slowly opened the album. The yellow pages were brittle due to age, and they were heavy with memories from Sarah's school days. As she looked into the first picture, she remembered how she cried all day on the first day of kindergarten and the day she met her friend Kayla. As she turned the pages, the memories from school played in her mind like a movie. She realised the important role Berkeley High has played in her life. She suddenly wanted to visit the school before she sold this old property; she moved to London and cut all ties with this city. She was a bit anxious at first, but she stood up quickly and dusted herself off, and looked at the album in her hand. She wiped the dust off the front cover and looked at her reflection on the glossy plastic wrap. As she zoned out and her mind whirred off to those sunlit chatty corridors of her school and

Dive into the past

the warmth of her teacher's voice, she smiled. She knew she had to visit one last time. She took the album with her and descended the stairs smiling like an idiot, thinking of all those warm Junior High memories. The house was once again left to its peaceful state of disturbing stillness. She got onto her car and swiftly drove off through her memory lane to the streets she knew like the back of her hand. She reached the school and got off the car. She went straight to the staff's room and knocked on the door before entering. Ms. Jonas's reading glasses were hanging on the tip of her nose for its dear life. Sarah felt like nothing had changed. MsJonas was startled, but she immediately recognised Sarah's voice. She took her glasses off and motioned Sarah to come and sit on the chair nearby. They talked for an hour about how their lives were, how Sarah is now a columnist and a full-time writer in the State's famous morning newspaper. Sarah then said her goodbye and went to see her grade 9 classroom, which was the first classroom on the second floor. The students have gone for their PE. She entered the classroom and looked around. New smart boards and desks looked crisp and neat. She looked at the artworks hung on the wall and the star performer's chart. She never liked those charts. She went and sat at the desk where she used to sit for her classes. From there looking front, so many things have changed. So many new chapters, so many people, so many relationships, so many paths have crossed, but the lessons your school teaches always set the right attitude to look at life. It brings together children

Dive into the past

from different fragments of the society and teaches us the strength in unity of such a cultural integration. The school silently sows the seed of humanity, wisdom, courage, leadership, creativity, and ethics in our minds. The most fertile minds accept it, nurture it and grow it into beautiful personality traits. Bearing the fruit from enduring and facing each situation with righteousness and fairness. The school does build responsible citizens. Sarah knew what her column would be on in the Monday morning newspaper. Sarah left the school with a lighter heart. She was happy she decided to visit one last time.

-   Joshni

Dive into the past

My lovable classroom

From: Slate pencil and Fragrance eraser
To: Note pad and Ink aroma
Subject: Kinder garden to Higher standard

My lovable classroom,

From the laziness of the sunrise,
To the happiness of the sunset;
The back bench chit chat hasn't failed to annoy the teacher.
Crazy joke's from friend's hasn't failed to burst out the laughter.
Interval breaks hasn't failed to give chance for chalk and duster clashes.
Surprise test hasn't failed to break the rhythm of the day.
Lunch boxes hasn't failed to bond the tummies of hunger.
Noon classes hasn't failed to boost us with short nap.
Maths class hasn't failed to engage the physical training class.
Exams hasn't failed to fill the anxiety.
Farewell hasn't failed to shed the tears of classroom.
Classrooms hasn't failed to load the memories.
My adorable teachers,

Your words, in the game of life,
"Go on, live your life,

Dive into the past

Pace up to the holy grail,
Taste the love of life"
Hits my back and pushes me forward;
You all made it simple,
To all my complications;
Your distinctive tranquil smile to my unetiquette
behaviour made my days;
You paved the strings of rainbows, when my mind
was on drift;
You showed me an obvious trait towards my tangled
and chaotic affairs;
This classroom with
both the hell and paradise of my soul,
Got conceited by your canning process;
Indicatingly, blackboard manifested the
Colourful chalk talk to my life.

My Dear friends,

The best part of my school life,
Yep! its you, I do remember,
From where my parents left my hand
To you, the one's holding it back;
All the anxiousness and worries faded when we were
together;
Can you rewind it?
We used to fall into laughter
Until our tummy hurts;
And those mischievous chuckling's amidst the
lecture;
From the day I passed out from school,
Felt like it's a surreal thing ,
That I believed in forever,

Dive into the past

But my heart mourned like December;
And now, my heart is persistent as like,
"Hey you, let's visit again for a while?
Like into the realms of fantasy".

-   DHARANI.R

Dive into the past

Truth Of School Life

School times end but memories won't. Yeah, I have finished my schooling before three years still remember that day, I gave my last answer sheet and left my hall. Tiny pencils to parker pens, broken crayons to brush pens, flat erasers to pelicans, waiting for a bell sound to mobile notification sound, narrating every event to our mother to keeping stuff to ourselves, we all came of age.14 years of journey flashed by. The next day I took my homework diary. I realised that it was supposed to be empty. I don't know why I still have a habit of writing my daily stuff in the diary and checking whether I completed it or not, winsome nah...

In the span of existence, school life is the finest pages of my life book with lots of scribblings. I literally never thought how much we would miss it after the finalization of schooling. I laugh at myself, recalling the day I was in school; how precious those moments are...? Of course, having some complicated responsibilities still reminds me of those homework days. The memories of one lunch box with many hands won't fade. Being or pretending to be a good girl or boy in the peep of teachers, we dreaded to share the answer sheets for a copy.

And many dreaded words in that life are "Call your parents," and "Who is your class teacher?". As Angela K. Bennett said, "Teaching middle school is

Dive into the past

an adventure not a job " Our teachers get through many struggles because of us and vice versa. Remember, we all get through that difficult state when our best-loved teacher is angry with us, when we really sick yet our parents made us go to school, but we slept on the last bench and escaped from all the boring lectures. Yeah, I really long for those sick days.

That time when our teacher asked us a question, but we had a toffee in our mouth, is a situation in which something unpleasant or dangerous could happen to us. And unforgettable moments like reading our first novel, which is better than our school books, surviving our first school dance, getting candy from our beloved teacher, getting good marks in our favorite subjects, the day when your last period was PT, bunking classes on both children's day and teacher's day, listening to teacher's personal story instead of important lessons... Haven't those moments come to your mind yet?

Boring uniforms, unadjustable classmates, many sections, one beloved friend, silly fights, group photos, combined studies, justified mistakes... No matter what we get through, our school memories always make us happy.

-   Ashwetha

-

Sometimes, it's better to bunk a class and enjoy with friends, because now, when I look back, marks never make me laugh, but memories do.

Dive into the past

The Magic Board

The Blackboard:

When I think about school, it is a treasure box filled with all my firsts, my first friend, first teacher, first embarrassing moment, first win, first lose, first myths, first facts, first blood, first gossip, first heartbreak, first slap, first kiss, first crush, and so many firsts—our world with our own rules inside this big universe of school. School life is divided into many phases; here are some of the phases.
The Doctor, Astronaut, Cricketer Phase:

This is the beginning phase of school. This is the phase in which we all secured full marks and asked the teacher for stars and V good. Cried if we lose marks in the exam (days to be smiled at ourselves). Teachers were God for us. Their approval means a lot to us. Class Leader will be like the King of the clan. His words were not words, those were orders, and we followed, no questions asked.

Everybody dreams of being either Doctor, Astronaut, Scientist, Cricketer, Teacher (Imagine what would have happened if that became a reality). Pure innocence was the gift of this phase. Cricket and Cartoons were the only topics to talk about. Spring Bat of Ricky Ponting, Undertaker's seven lives, was

Dive into the past

the first myth of our lives. Friends with Flora pencil and scented rubber were considered richest, and friends with 'Classmate' note considered wisest.

Boys and girls friendships were pure. Every boy will have a girl competitor in scoring marks (those were the days when boys were as good as girls in studies)—made to sit together without any hesitation. Pulling hair and pushing from the bench, all we had was some harmless(!) fun. Eager to use ink pens as we pass on to the next grades. Boys switching from trousers to pants and girls switching from skirts to churidar happen at the end of this phase.

The Lofatuation Phase:

For most people, school life is the place for first love. When we talk about 'The Blackboard', love is inevitable. School love is also called puppy love. Personally, I would never call this puppy love as 'love.' I would also never consider it as infatuation. It is something that is less than love and more than an infatuation. There is no name to call this phenomenon. So, I would call this 'Lofatuation.' Whenever we hear the word school life, this is the phase that strikes our mind.

This is the most beautiful phase of school life. You will be in the hangover of the hormones. You will find a reason to go to school. Marks start to reduce.

Dive into the past

Cheeks start to pain, on smiling from teeth to teeth for the whole day. Eyes became a camera that autofocuses her amidst her friends. There will be a friend. There will always be a friend with you who says, "Hey, she is looking and smiling at you." Those eight words will give the energy to work for the eight hours of school.

Stalking seems scary, not to social media stalking, the real, in-person stalking. The boy will be on the left row, and the girl will be on the right row, and the blackboard will be front. A perfect skill is developed so that it looks like the boy looks at the board, but he looks at the girl with the corner of his eye.

If the girl is from the other class, then break hours are the only window to see her. Walking across the corridor for infinite times and looking for her through the windows. A simple eye contact makes your day 100 times better. Class photos were the only way of talking her home with you. This phase is not graded specifically can happen at any grade. Most of the lofatuation phase ends in separation. Separation due to time, maturity, or rejection. But the most amazing phase in School life.

The bonding phase:

This phase here is about the lunch hour and P.T hour. In our school, during lunch, students can sit

Dive into the past

anywhere on the campus. Finding a spot that has shade under a tree is like getting tickets for FDFS. After finding the spot, the feast begins. If somebody's lunch is poori or noodles, then that person must leave the class with an empty stomach. There is no 'sharing' of lunch; there will be 'snatching' of lunch. There will always be a vegetarian friend, who funnily argues that meal maker is as equal as chicken and gets roasted like a chicken by other friends. The days after Ramzan, or Christmas, or Diwali will be awesome. Friend's parents will be packing separate boxes for everybody, and it will be a festival for us. In the 45 minutes of lunch, eating will be for 15 minutes, and laughing will be for 30 minutes. There is a theory that 'people who bond over food never separates,' and my friends are the proof of it.

The P.T period, the period for which we wait for a whole week. From forming a line to going from class to the ground and standing with one arm's distance, everything is exciting. We will be ready to get the ball and start to play, but the MASTER will have other ideas, 'run around the ground five times.' After these 20 exhausting minutes of running, there will be another 10 minutes of warm-up. Followed by random shouting of 'attention' and 'stand at ease.' Then there will be checking for big fingernails and long hair; if you get caught, get ready to get your knuckles hurt. After all, this sir will permit to take the ball. Shouting before serves to get the girls'

Dive into the past

attention and voluntarily throwing the ball to girls' side and collecting it as a hero, we all waited for those moments. If two classes have the same P.T period, then it's war. From intense planning and failed execution to last-minute points, our bonds grew in this game very much.

The Machine Phase:

This Phase can be a little bad and even traumatic phase for many. The Machine phase. This happens at the later period of school life, where a student is requested to study hard. That's it.

The ambitions of the first phase are killed, and now new ambitions are made, like scoring good marks and joining an engineering college of good rank or to join an art and science college. Rarely do some students save their ambition and nourish it in this phase.

The hangover of the second phase seizes and just becomes a memory. Rarely do some students hold on to that phase a little longer.

Tuitions become a second home, and tests become our new companions. Free times find a tiny hole in the whole timetable. The board exams become boring exams. Each and every minute has its minute significance in the preparation.

Dive into the past

This is the phase where friends and friendship play an important role. All those years of developing friendships in school will help you in this phase. The journey of this phase will be tough, but you will have good people to make this a little easy.

These are just some of the phases of the school. Even if there are both good and bad school memories, if given an opportunity to relive those moments, we never say no. That's the magic of 'The Blackboard'.

- Aravindh R

Dive into the past

Co-authors

Aravindh R— I am currently pursuing my final year in my Bachelors in Engineering degree and soon to be a software engineer. I am new to writing stuff. To write something, inspiration is required, and for that, the print medium was never my cup of tea. I get my inspiration from a visual medium. In fact, I haven't read a single book in my life, but I have written a book.

The moment when we put the last full stop to our work gives me a satisfaction that nothing can give. Writing needs a lot of thinking. I think 'thinking' opened a lot of new perspectives on life. It made me a better person. Here is my take on a version of 'The Blackboard'.

Dharani - A Commerce student and a budding writer by passion who enjoys wording the moments of life.

Dive into the past

Ashwetha - I'm pursuing my bachelor's degree in computer application. I want to pursue a master's in Business administration. Being a linguaphile, I love to learn new words and things. The John Burroughs saying "Leap and the net will appear" was brought me here. fingers crossed. And I'm a tremendous fan of Paulo Coelho.

Ram Mohan- An Engineer by profession but writer by choice has started writing poems in Tamil and English during his teenage. He quoted, "I find happiness every time while arranging distinct words in order to express my feelings and views to the outside world." His writings are not so exquisite, but it has a strong meaning that connects with the actual emotion of a commoner. You can share your views with him on rammohanwrites@gmail.com and find in Instagram as ram_mohan__.

Dive into the past

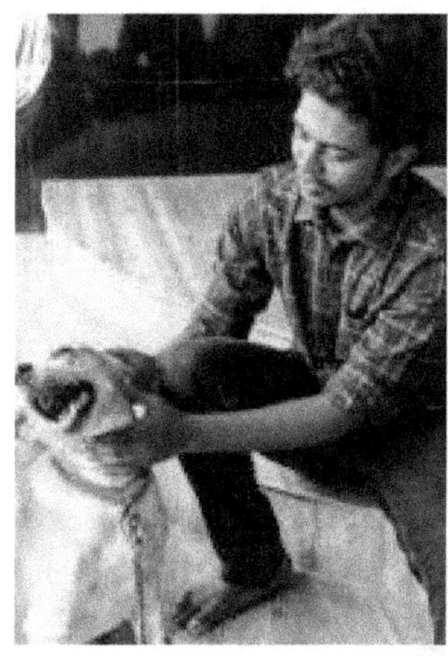

Nagapranith- A student pursuing medicine, who strives to live every bit of life thats out there.

Who feels at home looking at the stars and finds peace in a coffee amidst a sunset breeze.

Loves to capture moments on paper that he knows... he'll look back in the future.

Nithese Krishna V.M. A 21-year-old young writer from Vellakoil, a town in Tirupur District, Tamil Nadu. I'm a B.com (Honors) Degree holder who graduated from CHRIST (Deemed to be University) Bangalore.

I'm the author of the novel 'An Angel's Story' & a short story collection 'Vasaganin Eluthu.' I started exploring books at the age of 17.

Think and Grow Rich was the book that made me follow my passion. I started a Youtube Channel (Pesum Nool) to share my book reading experiences with the audience.

I love writing, and I'm continuing it.

Dive into the past

Sandra- A 20 yr old from Kerala, currently engaged in dentistry, savouring the freedom of expression through words. Favourite pastimes include chess, pop music, and reading books. Believes nothing is more important than hunting and relishing your true self.

Saranika- She is pursuing her bachelor's degree final year in a well-developed institution, where she develops an excellent knowledge in English, and her interest in English makes it her passion, and she works for it. She feels it is the way to show her individuality.

Dive into the past

Surya- I'm B.com Honours Graduate from Christ University, Bangalore. I am working as an audit assistant at a firm. When I write, I am being myself. I am not acting fake in my words.

Hari Prakaash R S- I have completed my Bachelors in Engineering. I had little interest in reading and writing for a long time. But the lockdowns and quarantine completely changed those habits. Being an introvert, reading took me to a whole new world and gave me company when I was alone and depressed. So I have decided to give a shot at my writing skills as well.

Dive into the past

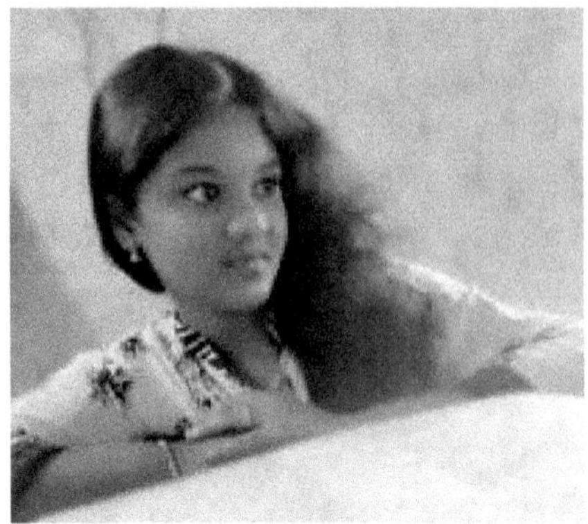

Yuvarani- I am currently doing my UG in dentistry. Sketching and painting always help in relaxing my mind. Books never fail to surprise me, where you come across various emotions. One can think that reading books is just a hobby. But it is more than what you predicted. The authors give life to the characters, but those characters can only survive in the reader's imagination which is entirely different from one another. Loves to scribble whatever my heart blabbers and wholly disappear into My World, which is a kind of magical realm.

Joshni Deivasigamani is renowned for her powerful wordplay. She plays and paints with words like its colours from a vibrant pallet. She takes inspiration from deeply felt emotions and composes them into unmethodical flash fictions or beautiful pieces of poetry. Her strength is her words.

Dive into the past

Shri Logitha- She is a student, admiring simplicity &still learning the subjects of school and life. An unconditional

Lover of life made her a perfect bibliophile. She listens a lot and evolves herself with kindness. Given the freedom to express herself, she has taken her first step regardless of consequences. She expresses humble gratitude for being a part of this great anthology. With this initial step, she sees a long path awaits her.

Gautham- I have currently completed my Bachelor's in Engineering. I have always been an admirer of the mindset of authors and poets, the way they express their views through words and is unique in their own perspective. Reading takes me to a different reality, and writing keeps me fantasized. This is my first work on a public platform, and I hope my words convey their intended meaning.

Dive into the past

Anjana- "Memories make minds like the stars make the sky. I'm just a girl who cherishes these beautiful stars in my sky, black or bright, gold or light."

Ms. Abitha Sivaraman - is studying 9th grade in Kendriya Vidyalaya, K.R. Puram, Bengaluru. She had won best Student of the Year 2012-2013 during her pre-primary schooling. She had participated in various co-curricular activities held in school & inter-school. In 2015-16, 2017-18, she won first place for English recitation. Also, she participated in the English recitation event held in 2016 at cluster level Bal Diwas co-curricular activities & Mini Sports

Dive into the past

meet held at Kendriya Vidyalaya, DRDO, Bengaluru. In the year 2018, she had participated in Swami Vivekananda Jayanti & National Youth oratorical contests. She secured the first rank in National English Indian Talent (NEIT) Competition, held at the school level, in the academic year 2016-17. She had participated in KVS 46th Jawaharlal Nehru National Science, Mathematics and Environment Exhibition 2019 and presented her science project on the theme "Health & Cleanliness." She had participated in KVS regional level 27th National Children's Science Congress-2019 and presented her project on the sub-theme "Traditional Knowledge System." She completed the YSL internship program last summer 2020, with extensive data collection about "Impact on environmental changes on butterfly biodiversity."

Aswathy P J

As the name goes by her star sign, her parents Jayarajan, a businessman, and Indu, a homemaker, who is an avid reader, had no difficulty naming her. As she grew up enjoying the aesthetics of shoranur and Mankara, the rural areas of Palakkad and Thrissur, enjoying the culture around it, she inherited a natural interest towards the books and the Library. As a student, she made the podium several times for her writings. When she found out the dancer in her, she explored her talents further into Classical dance. And that's how she spent a lot of her leisure time, either by being a Book worm, immersed in the world of Books, or trying a few steps in dancing for her favorite songs. Friendly in nature and a chatterbox, she also loves to travel with friends and explore new places, especially the places she knows through the books like the Thasrak. Mayyazhi is one of the dream places to visit that is on her bucket list! Currently pursuing BDS in Chennai, she never left her interest in Poetry and writings. Her poems and words dig deeper into her own reflections as a human being and the nostalgias she enjoyed growing up. Mole is one such tale that emphasis the fight of a girl or a woman against society and its norms, her struggles to come out of the social constructs around her by empowering herself. Mole is a bold attempt to break down the barriers to opportunity and to build confidence by educating yourself. An endeavour of being a Blackboard that literally lets all the letters that fall on it shine brighter!

M.ARCHITHA SUVI

ON MY TRACK TO PURSUE MA ENGLISH LITERATURE... WHO ALWAYS FELL IN LOVE WITH DEPTH OF WORDS AND PHRASES, THAT KEEPS ME WRITING!! WORDS HAVE THE POWER TO HEAL AND HURT, AND I WISH TO HEAL THE WORLD THROUGH MY WORDS. EVER SINCE I STARTED TO WRITE, LIFE HAS BECOME LIGHT-WEIGHTED; THAT'S WHAT WORDS DO.

Dive into the past

TRYING MY FULLEST TO USE BEAUTIFUL WORDS IN ORDER TO MAKE LIFE A BETTER PLACE TO LIVE IN.

Dive into the past

Special Gratitude

Special thanks to the publication

@Noellorenzbooks- NOEL LORENZ HOUSE OF FICTION

THEY ARE ASSOCIATED WITH TOP BOOK LIBRARIES ACROSS INDIA AND THE WORLD. IT IS A FABULOUS PLATFORM FOR EVERY BUDDING WRITER. ITS MISSION IS TO EMPOWER WRITERS, THINKERS, AND CREATIVE ARTISTS TO DISTRIBUTE HIGH-QUALITY CONTENT THROUGHOUT THE WORLD.

NLHF — THE PUBLISHER WITH ALL FREE BOOKS IN MULTIPLE WORLD RECORDS.

KRIPPASHINI'S SPECIAL THANKS AND WISHES TO NLHF!

Dive into the past

~End~

Dive into the past

www.noellorenz.com

Dive into the past